TREASURE TRAIL

MO

BUZZ

SNICKER

RIFF

WHEEZY

FARMER FI

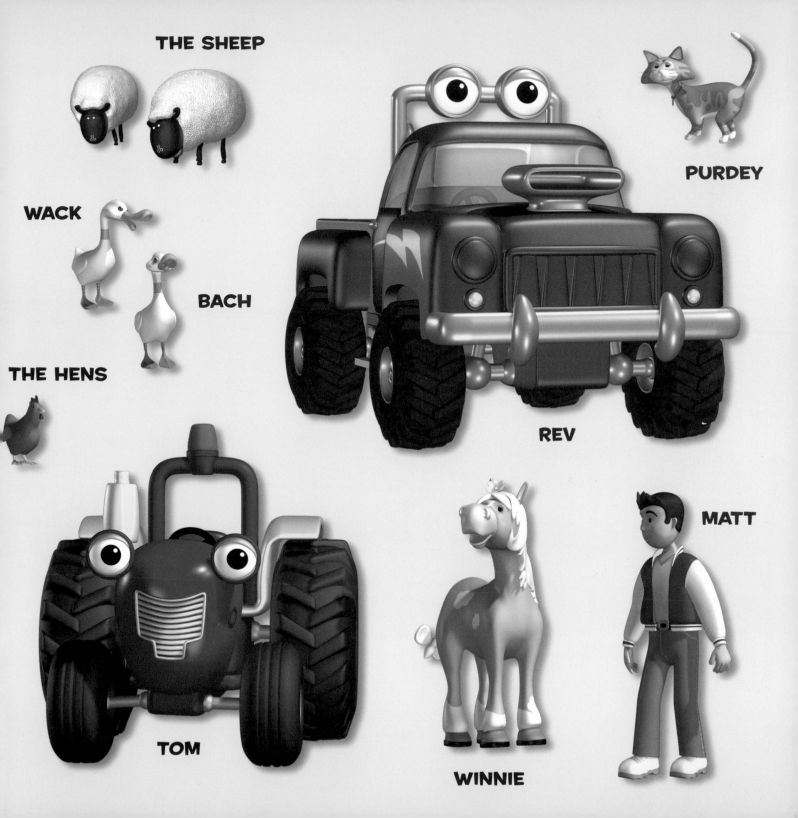

THE SHEEP

PURDEY

WACK

BACH

THE HENS

REV

TOM

WINNIE

MATT

First published in Great Britain by HarperCollins Children's Books in 2004

1 3 5 7 9 10 8 6 4 2

ISBN: 0-00-718900-1

Text adapted from the original script by Chris Trengrove

The Contender Entertainment Group
48 Margaret Street, London, W1W 8SE

Tractor Tom © Contender Ltd 2002

TREASURE TRAIL

An imprint of HarperCollins*Publishers*

Everybody at Springhill Farm was very excited.
That night, Fi was having a bonfire party.

Tom had one little job to do – take an old
cupboard and put it on the bonfire. Fi thought
she had better check there was nothing inside
it first.

When she came to the last drawer, Fi found
some old photos.

"This is my grandad. He was a soldier,
you know!" said Fi, pointing to one
of the photos.

"Just look at all his medals!
He must have been really
brave!" she said proudly.

Matt was getting ready to spend the morning on his new hobby.

"It's a metal detector, Rev," he explained, as he switched on the machine.

"You use it to look for metal things."

"Bonggg!" went the machine, as it clanked onto Rev's bonnet!

"Oops, sorry, Rev!" said Matt. "I must have had it turned up too high."

Tom and Fi took the old cupboard to put it on the bonfire.

But when Tom broke it up,
Fi noticed something.
"Hang on – what's that?" wondered Fi.
It was a mysterious box.

"It's locked and I can't open it," she said.
"I'll try again later when I have time."

Later, when Fi had gone to have lunch, Buzz, Wheezy and Tom tried to open the box for her.

They tried everything but it just wouldn't open.

They did find something on the bottom of it though – a set of initials and a keyhole!

Matt thought he had found some treasure with the metal detector.

But it wasn't gold coins or a diamond ring. It was an old bath! Rev couldn't help laughing, then Tom joined in, and then the sheep started! Baa ha ha ha ha!

"Well, I'm off," sulked Matt. "And you can do what you like with that silly, rotten, smelly old bath!" So off the sheep went to play with the bath.

Back at the barn, Wheezy and Buzz
were showing Fi what they
had found.

"These are my
grandad's initials!"
cried Fi. "The box
must have belonged
to him! And look, there's
a keyhole!"

Fi shook the box. They could hear
something clinking inside!

"Oh, if only we knew where the key was!"
she said.

Then Tom had an idea...

Tom thought the key might be somewhere in the broken bits of old cupboard on the bonfire.

But it was like looking for a needle in a haystack. Poor Tom didn't find anything.

Later that day, Matt was surprised to see the rusty old bath moving.
"Help, I'm being chased by an old tin bath. Tom, save me!" shouted Matt, tripping over Tom!

But when Tom lifted the upside down bath it was only a SHEEP underneath!
"Hey! What's all the noise about? I thought this was supposed to be a bonfire party!" said Fi.

The fireworks at the bonfire party were fantastic but Tom was rather sad. He was sure that the key to the mysterious box was now lost forever somewhere in the bonfire. Or was it?

Tom had another idea! He bobbed up and down with excitement. But it would have to wait until the next day.

The next morning, Tom went back to the ashes of
the bonfire with Matt and the metal detector.

"You want me to look for treasure HERE,
Tom?" asked Matt.
Just then, the metal detector began to
beep loudly.

"Hang on, what's
this?" said Matt,
hooking out a key!

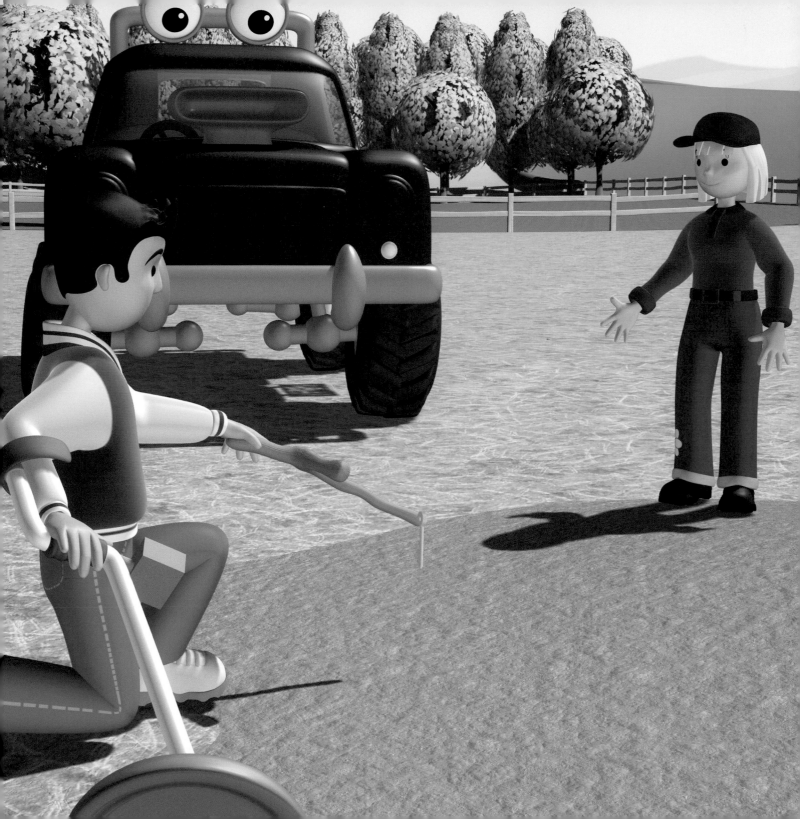

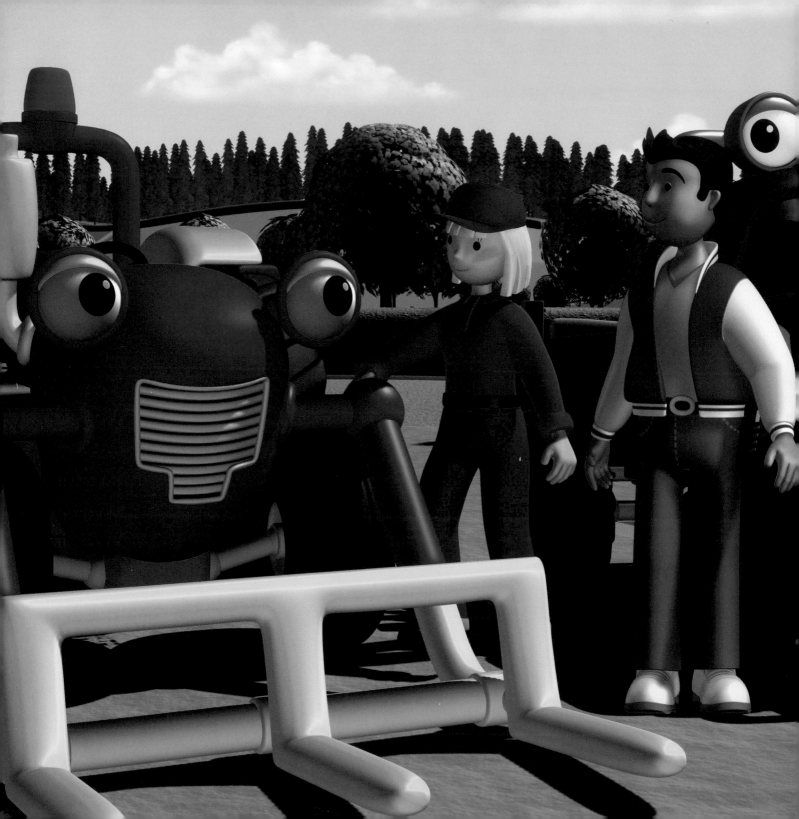

Fi put the key into the box's lock and turned it.
Inside was a set of golden medals!

"Look, Matt. Much better than treasure –
grandad's medals!" said Fi excitedly.

"Well, at least my metal
detector turned out to
be some use," said
Matt happily. "But it
was Tom's idea,
you know."

"Tom, you've saved the
day again. What would I do
without you?" smiled Fi.

MO

BUZZ

SNICKER

RIFF

WHEEZY

FARMER FI

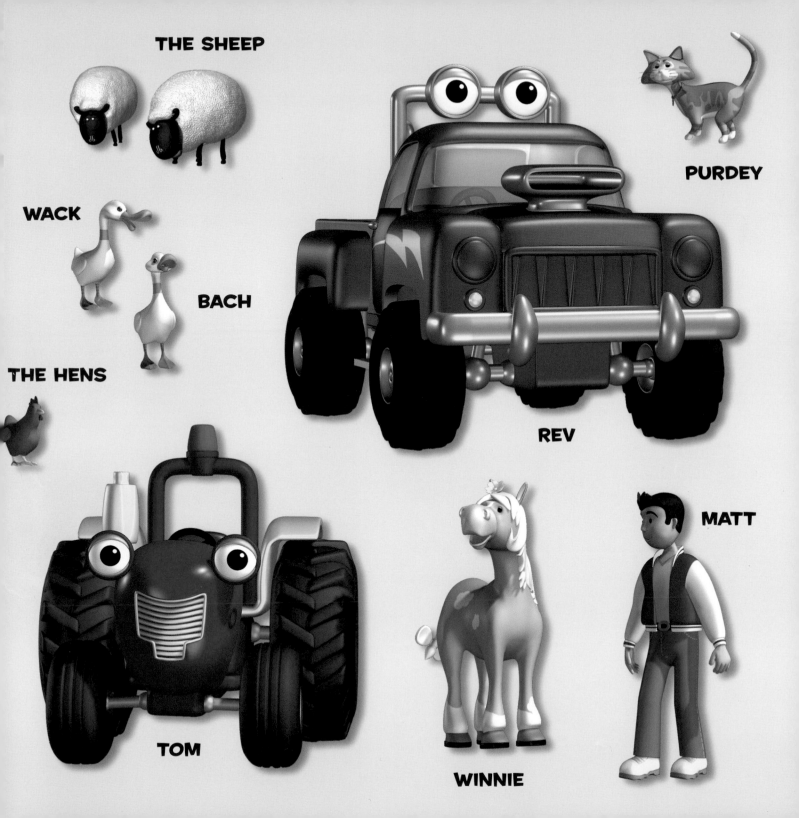

THE SHEEP

WACK

BACH

THE HENS

PURDEY

REV

TOM

WINNIE

MATT

YOU CAN COLLECT THEM ALL!

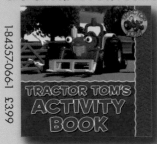

1-84357-066-1 £3.99

TRACTOR TOM'S ACTIVITY BOOK

1-84357-064-5 £3.99

TRACTOR TOM AND THE MOBILE PHONE

1-84357-065-3 £3.99

TRACTOR TOM'S "WHERE'S IT GONE?" STICKER BOOK

1-84357-087-4 £3.99

TRACTOR TOM'S SPORTS DAY

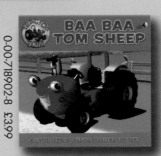

0-00-718904-4 £5.99

MY TRACTOR TOM PLAYBOOK

FIND AND FIT THE SHAPES TO HELP TRACTOR TOM ON THE FARM!

0-00-718900-1 £3.99

TREASURE TRAIL

0-00-718901-X £3.99

A SURPRISE FOR FI

0-00-718902-8 £3.99

BAA BAA TOM SHEEP

0-00-718903-6 £3.99

A JOB FOR BUZZ

CAN TOM BE FIXED IN TIME TO SAVE THE DAY?

TRACTOR TOM

WHAT WOULD WE DO WITHOUT HIM?